DATE		
WITHDRAWN		
WITHDRAWN		

MATT CHRISTOPHER®

#5
ROCK ON

Text by Stephanie Peters
Illustrated by Michael Koelsch

LITTLE, BROWN AND COMPANY

New York ᠊ᢑ᠊ Boston

Little, Brown and Company

Time Warner Book Group
1271 Avenue of the Americas, New York, NY 10020
Visit our Web site at www.lb-kids.com

First Edition

The characters and events portrayed in this book are fictitious.
Any similarity to real persons, living or dead, is coincidental
and not intended by the author.

Matt Christopher® is a registered trademark
of Catherine M. Christopher.

Library of Congress Cataloging-in-Publication Data
Peters, Stephanie True.
Rock on / Matt Christopher ; text by Stephanie Peters ;
illustrated by Michael Koelsch. — 1st ed.
p. cm. — (The extreme team ; #5)
Summary: X's friends believe he can excel at any extreme sport, so when
they want to check out the new climbing wall at the mall, he decides to
hide his fear of heights rather than have them think him a coward.
ISBN 0-316-76265-2 (pb) / ISBN 0-316-76264-4 (hc)
[1. Rock climbing — Fiction. 2. Courage — Fiction. 3. Fear — Fiction.]
I. Christopher, Matt. II. Koelsch, Michael, ill. III. Title. IV. Series.
PZ7.P441833Rl 2004   2003023755
[Fic] — dc22

10 9 8 7 6 5 4 3 2 1

PHX (hc)

COM-MO (pb)

Printed in the United States of America

CHAPTER ONE

"X! Wait up!"

Xavier McSweeney, or X to his friends and family, turned to see Mark Goldstein hurrying up the snow-covered hill. He stopped so his friend could catch up.

"I've been chasing you for five minutes!" Mark gasped. He stuck his snowboard in a snowbank, removed his glasses, and wiped his brow.

"Well, you caught me," X said. "What's up?"

"I need your help," Mark answered. He pointed to his snowboard. "That thing keeps turning sideways when I go downhill. I think there's something wrong with it. Can you check it out?"

X jammed his own snowboard into the bank. He

picked up Mark's board and looked it over. He handed it back to Mark with a shrug.

"Looks okay to me," he said. "Are you sure it's the board that's causing the trouble?"

Mark frowned. "Whaddya mean?"

X picked up his own board and started up the hill again. "I'm thinking maybe it's operator error. C'mon, take a run. I'll watch you, see if you're doing something wrong."

Mark sighed. "Okay, but I'm telling you, it's the board, not me."

The boys reached the top of the hill. Mark strapped himself on to his board, gave a little hop, and set off down the slope. His run started out smoothly. But halfway down, the tail of the board began sliding forward. Mark pinwheeled his arms to try to stay upright, but he wound up rolling in the snow. X took off down the hill and swooped to a stop next to him.

"See what I mean?" Mark fumed as they hurried

out of the way of the other boarders. "This stupid thing has a mind of its own!"

X sat down. "Got some bad news for you, bud," he said solemnly. "It's not the board. It's your technique."

Mark threw up his hands. "Okay, I give up. What's wrong with my technique, O Great One?"

"Lots." X stood up and pretended to ride a snowboard. "When you ride, you've got to put more of your weight forward." Knees bent, he leaned so that his arms dangled a little ahead of his front foot. "If your weight is on the back foot" – he shifted his arms and upper body backward – "then the heavy stuff is on the tail."

Mark shrugged. "So?"

"So," X said patiently, "the end of the board that has more weight on it goes down the hill first. It's, like, the law of gravity or something."

"But if I put my weight forward, I won't be able to move my front foot. How will I steer?"

X stared at Mark in disbelief. "Hello? Excuse me?

Where did you learn to board?" When Mark's face looked blank, X shook his head. "You don't steer a snowboard with your *front* foot, you steer with your *back* foot!"

"You do?" Mark seemed so amazed that X began to laugh.

"Let's head back up the hill. I'll show you what I mean."

"I got a better idea," a new voice behind them mocked. "Why don't you posers get out of the way and let some *real* snowboarders have the slope!"

CHAPTER TWO

X and Mark turned to find two boys and a girl standing in front of them. X immediately recognized the boy who had spoken. His name was Frank. X had met him a few months earlier when Frank's team faced X and his friends in a game of roller hockey. Before the game, Frank had made a bet with X's friend Belicia "Bizz" Juarez. The winning team would be able to use the skatepark's roller-hockey rink whenever they wanted. Before X and the others could stop her, Bizz had accepted the challenge.

Frank's team won the game. He'd been nasty then, full of himself and gloating about the victory. He didn't seem much better now.

Mark glared at them. "Who are you calling posers?"

Frank smirked. "You, for one. I saw you rollin' down the windows on that last run." Frank flailed his arms wildly, imitating Mark trying to keep his balance. His friends guffawed.

Mark flushed. "Okay, I admit I'm not the best boarder in the world," he said. "But X could outrun you in a second!"

Frank raised an eyebrow. "Wanna bet?"

Those were the same words Frank had used to trap Bizz. Before Mark made the same mistake, X stopped him. "No bets," he said.

"Too chicken?" Frank and his friends flapped their arms and clucked. "I dare you to race me down the hill!"

X narrowed his eyes. He'd seen Frank snowboard a few times before; he was pretty sure he could take him. "You're on!" he said.

They climbed to the top of the slope and met Alison Lee, the teenager who oversaw the skatepark and the hill. X explained Frank's challenge and asked for her help in clearing the hill for a few minutes.

Alison shook her head. "X, you know you're a good snowboarder. You don't have to race to prove it."

"I know," said X. He lowered his voice. "But he dared me. If I didn't race, he'd think I was a coward."

"So why do you care what he thinks?"

X didn't answer. Alison rolled her eyes, but she helped clear the hill. As she did, a small crowd gathered at the top.

"Hey, what's the holdup?" Jonas Malloy pushed through to where X and Mark were standing.

"Yo, Jonas, you're just in time. X is going to race Frank down the hill," Mark said.

"No way!" Jonas threw an arm around X's shoulders. "Doesn't Frank know that X is the best boarder around?"

"Well, I wouldn't say —," X began.

"And not just the best boarder," Jonas continued in a loud voice. "He can ride anything on wheels, he rocks in the half-pipe *and* on the rails, and when it

9

comes to jammin' down a mountain on a bike, he's the boss! You look up *extreme sports* in the dictionary, you'll find a picture of X!" Jonas and Mark high-fived each other. Some of the kids in the crowd cheered. Frank and his buddies frowned.

X felt his face turn red. He wished Jonas hadn't said all those things. Now if he lost, he'd look like a total idiot!

CHAPTER THREE

It was too late to back out of the race — not that X wanted to. He crouched down, eyes glued to Alison.

"On your mark, get set, go," Alison said — and the race was on!

X launched himself into a straight downhill ride. His arms were low and forward, steadying him as he shot past the onlookers. His back foot worked to keep the board in line. He didn't look to see where Frank was. He focused on staying in control and making it down the hill as fast as he could.

Suddenly, a mound of snow appeared in front of him. X didn't have time to go around it. Instead, he bent his knees and hit the mound at full speed.

Airborne, he grabbed his board with one hand. As he started to fall, he let go and shifted his weight to his back foot. The last thing he wanted was for the nose of the board to dig into the snow and send him flying.

Thud! His landing was hard but clean. Seconds later, he skidded to a stop at the bottom of the hill. Panting, he turned just in time to see Frank finish his run. X gave a *whoop* and pumped his fist in the air. He'd won!

Frank shot X a mean look, unsnapped his bindings, and stalked away. His friends joined him. The girl tried to put an arm around his shoulders, but Frank shook it off angrily.

A spray of snow showered X in the back as first Jonas, then Mark boarded up beside him.

"That was the most beautiful run this hill has ever seen," Mark said solemnly.

"I could not *believe* how you stuck that jump!" Jonas cried. "I thought for sure you were going to crater. But no, you boosted about five feet into the air instead!"

X grinned. "Thanks, guys. It felt pretty good, I gotta admit. But now that the excitement's over, let's go back to normal, okay?"

"I don't think it's going to be that easy." Alison joined them. She jerked her thumb at Frank and his friends. "You've just made yourself a real enemy, X. And it's my guess that he's going to try to find a way to get back at you." She picked up her board and started up the slope. Then she stopped.

"Hey, I almost forgot. There's a new rock-climbing wall set up at the mall. It's two stories high. I'm getting a trip together to check it out. If you guys want to go, sign up at the Community Center. But do it soon because I can only take ten kids."

"A rock-climbing trip? Totally awesome!" Jonas said after Alison had left. "C'mon, you guys, let's go sign up."

"I don't know," X said doubtfully. "I've never been rock climbing. And in the mall? How do they do that?"

x

14

"I've seen something like it before," Mark replied. "The wall is man-made, out of heavy-duty plastic or something, and has handholds and footholds sticking out of it. You get strapped into a safety harness attached to a rope. Then you just, you know, climb as high as you can. When you let go of the wall, the harness takes you to the floor safely."

"So is it hard to do?" X wanted to know.

Jonas laughed. "What do you care if it's hard? You're good at everything! This wall will be a cinch for you!"

"Yeah, right," X replied. Despite Jonas's confidence, he wasn't so sure.

CHAPTER FOUR

There were only two names on the sign-up sheet so far: Bizz Juarez and Savannah Smith. Mark laughed when he saw them.

"Looks like Alison already told Bizz and Savannah about the trip!" he said. He added his own name beneath theirs, then handed the pen to Jonas. Jonas scrawled his name and stepped away so X could do the same.

X hesitated. "You know, it doesn't seem fair for us to take up all the spaces. What if some other kid wants to go but can't because I signed up instead? My mom could always take me some other time." He started to put the pen down.

Jonas wouldn't let him. "It won't be as much fun if you don't go with us," he said. "Besides, these trips are always first come, first served."

So X signed his name underneath Jonas's and laid the pen aside. They all took copies of the permission slip for their parents to sign and started to leave.

"Hold on. What about Charlie?" Mark asked. Charlie Abbott was another friend. "Should we put his name down, too?"

"I don't think we're allowed to," Jonas said. "I'll call him later, tell him to get his keister over here pronto."

"He could always take my place if he doesn't get on the list," X said.

Jonas gave him a puzzled look. "If I didn't know any better, I'd say you didn't want to go on this trip!"

X was saved from having to answer by a cry from Mark.

"Hey, it's almost three-thirty! Alison's going to close the hill soon. If we want to get in any more runs, we better get a move on!"

The boys snowboarded for another half hour before the sun set and Alison had to shut down the hill. X waved good-bye to his friends and trudged home with his snowboard under his arm. He was tired and aching, but he barely noticed. He was too busy thinking about what Jonas had said – that he, X, didn't want to go on the trip.

X was as mystified by his reluctance as Jonas was. Usually, he was ready and raring to try new things, especially new sports. But every time he thought of climbing straight up a wall, his insides felt funny.

He dumped his snowboard in the garage when he got home, then pushed open the door to the kitchen. Delicious smells tickled his nose. His favorite meal, spaghetti with meatballs, was warming on the stove. X's older sister, Ruth, was setting the table like she did every night. X's job was to make sure each place had a glass of milk by it. He pulled the milk from the refrigerator, then stopped short.

"Hey, where are the glasses?" he asked Ruth.

"In the dishwasher," she replied. "Mom forgot to run it again. She was too busy playing with Sarah and Kyle."

X laughed. His mother would rather play with her kids than do housework. It meant that their house was messy sometimes, but X didn't care. What fun was a mom who just cleaned all day?

"So what should I use for the milk?" X asked.

Ruth pointed to a small cupboard above the refrigerator. "I think there are some plastic cups up there," she said.

X pulled himself onto the counter. He couldn't quite reach the cupboard, so he climbed up on top of the refrigerator.

"Careful you don't fall!"

X glanced down — and froze. Suddenly, the floor seemed to be very far away.

CHAPTER FIVE

Panic washed over X. A wave of dizziness struck him. He squeezed his eyes shut, hoping to make it stop. It didn't. He lost his balance and started to fall.

"X! Watch out!" Ruth screamed.

X braced himself for the pain. But instead of hitting hard tile, he landed in his father's strong arms.

"Gotcha!" Mr. McSweeney held X in a tight hug for a moment, then helped him to a chair. "What happened?"

"I — I don't know," X croaked, still shaky. "One minute I was reaching for the cupboard, the next it was like I couldn't breathe!"

X's father looked at him thoughtfully. "Have you ever felt that way before?" he asked.

X probed his memory. "Well, there was the time the Ferris wheel stopped and I was in the top car. I was a little scared then, too, but just because the car wouldn't stop rocking."

"How about the time we were sitting in the balcony at the theater?" Ruth put in. "Jonas was sitting down below, calling and waving like crazy up at X. But X just sat there, staring straight ahead with his hands white-knuckling the arms of the seat. What does it mean, Dad?"

"I'm not one hundred percent sure," Mr. McSweeney replied, "but I think X was experiencing acrophobia."

"Acro-*what?*" X said.

"Acrophobia. The fear of heights. Lots of people have it."

X frowned. "Hold on a second. If I've got this acro-whatever thing, why don't I feel it when I'm up on a hill or waiting on deck at the half-pipe?"

His father shrugged. "Maybe it's because you're too busy thinking about the run you're about to take or the jumps you're going to do. Or maybe you're so familiar with those places the fear doesn't hit you." He patted X on the back. "Don't worry. If you stay away from unfamiliar heights, you shouldn't be bothered by it." He left to call the rest of the family to dinner.

When everyone was together, Ruth told the others about X's near accident. "If it hadn't been for Dad, X's brains would be splashed all over this very floor."

"Ew!" squealed Kyle and Sarah together.

"Ruth!" X's mother said. "That's not a very nice image for the dinner table."

Ruth grinned at X. "Sorry, Mom," she said.

X grinned back, but weakly. Ruth had meant to be funny, but what she'd said had made X uneasy. After all, his brains really *could* have been splashed all over the floor if not for his dad. He decided then and there to stay away from strange high places, just to be safe.

At that moment, the phone rang. X answered it.

"Hey, buddy!" Jonas said. "Good news. Charlie got the last spot on the sign-up sheet. So mark your calendar, get your permission slip signed, and get ready to climb that rock wall next week!"

CHAPTER SIX

"Who was that?" X's mother wanted to know after X hung up. He told her it was Jonas and explained about the trip. Then he pulled the permission slip out of his pocket and asked her to sign it.

She shook her head. "I don't know, X. Given your fear of heights, do you really think it's a good idea to try to climb the wall?"

X looked at his feet. "I've got to, Mom," he mumbled.

She lifted his chin with her hand and gazed into his eyes. "Why?" she asked softly.

"Because if I don't go, my friends will think I'm a coward!" he blurted out.

His mother continued to look at him. Then she released his chin and signed the slip.

"There are different kinds of bravery, you know," she said as she handed him the paper.

X folded the slip in half. "What do you mean?"

His mother stood up and ruffled his hair. "You'll figure it out. Now go hop in the shower and get ready for bed."

X did as he was told. But even though he was tired from snowboarding all day, he had trouble getting to sleep that night. Every time he closed his eyes, he remembered how scared he'd been on top of the refrigerator, a place that wasn't even all that high!

And now, in less than a week, he'd be climbing a two-story rock wall. The very idea gave him goose bumps. He pulled his comforter up to his chin and tried to figure out what to do. But he couldn't think of a single solution.

Maybe, he thought, *something will come up to keep me from going on the trip!*

* * *

At breakfast the next morning, X checked the family calendar to see if he was scheduled for a doctor or dentist appointment on Saturday. He wasn't. At school that week, he kept hoping his teacher would assign a big project for the class to complete over the weekend. She didn't. At the skatepark hill, he prayed for something to happen to keep Alison from doing the trip. Nothing did. And before he knew it, it was Saturday morning and he was boarding the minibus for the mall.

"This is going to be so great!" Jonas said as he bounced in the seat in front of X. "I wonder how high we go? I can't wait to see what the mall looks like from way up there."

Bizz snorted from the next seat. "It probably looks the same as it does when you look over the railing from the second floor."

X had only been half-listening to the conversation, but now he sat up. He tried to think if he'd ever looked over the second-floor railing before. He couldn't quite remember. *But I've been to the mall so*

many times, I must have! And I never got scared then, so maybe I'll be okay after all!

"You know, Bizz, I bet you're right!" he said excitedly. "I bet it's *exactly* like looking over the railing!"

Bizz looked at him with surprise. "Steady there, X," she said. "It's not like I just discovered the meaning of life or something."

X sat back, smiling for the first time that day. "Maybe not," he said. "But I still think you're a genius."

CHAPTER SEVEN

"Okay, guys, stay together," Alison said as they climbed off the minibus. "I came here with ten kids, so I gotta go home with ten."

She led the group through the mall. Suddenly, the rock wall loomed in front of them. It was just like Mark had described — two stories high with lots of bumps for hands and feet. There were three climbing areas. Thick red ropes dangled from the top of the wall at each area.

X's heart raced as he gazed up at the wall. It looked much higher than he'd expected. *Much* higher.

A tall teenage boy came forward and knocked fists with Alison. "Guys, this is my buddy Ben. He works here. He's going to tell you all about climbing the wall. So get in line, and have your money ready," Alison advised.

X put his hand in his pocket and fingered the five-dollar bill his mother had given him that morning. *Maybe I can pretend I lost it,* he thought. Then he saw Jonas give the attendant a ten-dollar bill and receive five back in change. He knew Jonas would give him that extra five if he thought X had lost his. With a sigh, he pulled out his money and handed it to Ben.

Ben led them into a circle of ropes around the wall and asked them to sit down. "Let me explain how this works. First, I strap you into a harness. The harness fits nice and snug around your upper legs and waist — kind of like a pair of underwear with no material!" He waited for them to stop laughing before going on. "Then I clip the harness onto a rope line. The rope, harness, and clips are very strong and very safe. They can support a person twice my size.

So they'll hold you up, no problem, even if you're swinging free of the wall. Last but not least, you get a safety helmet. Any questions?"

No one had any.

"You'll do the easy climb today," Ben said. "I'll be right there to point out places to put your hands and feet, but it will be up to you and your muscles to pull you to the next spot. You all look strong, though." He smiled. "When you reach the top, grab hold of the rope, just above the harness, and let your feet dangle free. The rope will slowly slide you back down to the floor. Now, who's first?"

Jonas jumped to his feet. Ben secured him in the harness, helped him put on the helmet, and led him to the wall. The harness was clipped to the rope with a loud click, and Jonas started to climb. Ben backed away as Jonas got higher and higher.

"You're doing great!" Ben called. Jonas looked down, let go with one hand, and gave a thumbs-up. Then he continued to feel for bumps until he'd reached the top.

"Hey, what's this for?" Jonas pointed to a large silver bell.

"Ring it to prove you made it to the top!"

Jonas grabbed the string attached to the bell's clapper and gave it a powerful yank. The bell clanged loudly. X and the others cheered. Jonas gripped the safety rope, pushed off from the wall, and did a slow free fall all the way to the floor. Ben unclipped him and helped him from the harness.

"That was way cool!" Jonas ran over to X. "Wait till you try it!"

X wished he could be as excited as Jonas. But as he stepped forward in line, all he felt was dread.

That dread deepened when he spied a group of kids standing just outside the ropes around the wall. In the midst of the group was Frank. He was staring right at X — and smiling the nastiest smile X had ever seen.

CHAPTER EIGHT

X tried to ignore Frank by watching Bizz climb the wall. She, too, made it safely to the top and rang the bell. Savannah was a little more cautious, but she didn't give up. Her smile was triumphant when she rang the bell. Then, suddenly, it was X's turn.

"Go, X!" Jonas cheered. Heart pounding, X stepped into the harness and put on the helmet. Ben led him to the wall and clipped him to the rope. X reached for the first handhold and placed a foot on a low bump. He pulled himself up.

This isn't so bad, he told himself as he reached for the next handhold. *I can do this.* He put his other foot on a bump and pulled up again.

I'm doing it! he thought. He climbed a bit higher.

"Great job!" Ben said.

X looked over his shoulder with a smile — a smile that froze on his face, then slowly slipped away when he saw how high up he was. He shut his eyes tightly, but it was too late. He knew at that moment there was no way he was going to ring the bell.

"X? Everything good?" Ben called.

X didn't answer. He was sure that if he opened his mouth, he would throw up. Instead, he clung to the side of the wall and listened to his heart knock in his chest.

Suddenly, he felt a hand on his calf. "Okay, X, just listen to me and you'll be fine." Ben's soft voice penetrated X's panicked brain. "First, take a deep breath. Then let go with one hand and grab the rope."

Slowly, X followed Ben's instructions.

"Perfect. Now the other hand. Good. Now just float downward. I'm right here the whole time."

After what seemed like an eternity, X touched the

floor. His legs and hands were shaking as Ben unclipped him and helped him out of the harness.

"Deep breaths, bud, slow deep breaths," Ben was saying. Alison had joined them. She put her hand on X's back to steady him. As X inhaled and exhaled he felt his heart slow and his shaking stop. Finally, he looked up.

The first thing he saw was Jonas staring at him, openmouthed with disbelief. Bizz, Savannah, Mark, and Charlie had similar expressions on their faces. X quickly looked away — and found himself locking eyes with Frank. Frank was grinning ear to ear.

And why shouldn't he? X thought bitterly. *He's just discovered that his enemy has a major weakness.*

"I — I think I'll go get a drink of water," X said. He ducked his head and made a beeline for the water fountain. As he bent over the stream of cool water, someone tapped him on the shoulder. It was Jonas.

"What happened up there?" Jonas wanted to know.

"I'll tell you what happened." Frank and his

friends sauntered up beside them. "Your hero here chickened out, that's what! He's afraid of heights!" Frank made clucking noises. His friends nudged each other and laughed.

"You guys are such nostril slugs," Jonas said. "X is not afraid of heights. He could climb that wall in a second if he wanted to." He pulled his remaining five-dollar bill from his pocket. "In fact, I've got a fiver here says he could do it right now! What do you say, X?"

But X didn't answer. The truth was, the last thing he wanted to do was go near the rock wall again. After a moment, Jonas put the money back in his pocket.

Frank clucked one last time, then walked away, his laughter ringing in X's ears.

CHAPTER NINE

On the bus ride home, X stared out a window, his knees drawn up under his chin. The other kids spoke in whispers. X felt their eyes on him from time to time, but no one said anything to him. When the bus dropped them off at the Community Center, X took off for home without a word.

His mother was outside shoveling their front steps. When she saw the look on X's face, she put the shovel aside and sat down.

"Didn't go so well, huh?" she said.

X's throat tightened and his eyes welled up. *Oh great,* he thought. *Now I'm going to cry. I'm not just a coward, I'm a baby, too!* He swallowed hard to make the lump in his throat go away.

Mrs. McSweeney patted the steps beside her. "Tell me what happened."

X shook his head.

"Please," his mother said. "You'll feel better if you get it out."

So X sat down and told her. The words came out in a rush. And to his surprise, he did feel better afterward.

His mother gave him a quick squeeze around the shoulders. "X, remember how I told you there are different kinds of bravery?"

X nodded.

"Well, today you showed one kind. You tried to climb that rock wall even though deep down you didn't want to."

"Yeah," X said dismally, "but I only got halfway up. Then I flipped out, and now Frank thinks I'm a coward." He picked up some snow and threw it at a nearby tree. It exploded with a puff of white, leaving

a smudge of snow behind on the bark. "And so do my friends."

His mother was quiet for a moment. Then she asked, "Why do you care what Frank thinks of you? From what you've told me about him, he seems like a bully."

X stared at her. She smiled.

"It takes another kind of bravery to ignore the mean things a bully says about you." She threw a snowball at the same tree, adding a second white mark beside X's. "Now let me ask you something else. Do you really think the fact that you only made it halfway up a fake rock-climbing wall will change what your best friends think about you?"

X threw another snowball and shook his head.

"Of course not," his mother agreed. "But if you have any doubts about it, why don't you call Jonas and explain what happened? I'll bet he and the others will think it was pretty awesome that you even tried the climb today." She grabbed her shovel and stood up.

"Telling people about your fears can be hard," she added. "But —"

X held up a hand. "Let me guess. That's another kind of bravery, right?"

"Right," she said with a grin. "Okay, enough lecturing for now. How about you scare up another shovel and help me out here?"

X got to his feet. He felt like a great weight had been removed from his shoulders. He started for the garage, then turned back.

"Thanks, Mom," he said.

"Anytime."

CHAPTER TEN

X cornered Jonas at school first thing the next morning and explained, as best he could, what had happened the day before. Jonas broke into a huge smile.

"Hooray, you're not perfect!" he said. "Being around perfect people is as boring as riding a mountain bike in a parking lot."

"So you and the others don't think I'm a coward?"

"Yeah, right," Jonas replied, rolling his eyes. "Get real, already, will you?" And that was the end of it.

That afternoon, X and his friends met up at the slope. "Isn't that Ben?" Jonas asked. Sure enough, there was the rock-climbing instructor, craning his neck as if looking for someone.

"Dudes!" he said as he spotted them. He knocked fists with each of them, then pulled X aside. "How you doin', Letterman?"

"Okay, I guess." X eyed the snowboard Ben was holding. "You know, I don't think I've ever seen you here before."

Ben shifted uncomfortably. "That's because I don't know how to board. But Alison invited me to come by, and I couldn't say no, you know? I've been standing here for fifteen minutes, trying to figure out a way to get down the hill before she gets here!"

X tried not to laugh. "Why don't you just tell her the truth when you see her?"

"The truth, huh? Lemme snack on that idea for a sec." Ben tapped his finger against his chin a few times, then smiled. "I got a better plan. How about you teach me how to board, and I'll help you get over your fear of the wall?"

X was caught off guard. "But — but learning to board takes time and practice. You can't learn it all at once."

Ben shrugged. "You can't get over a fear of heights all at once, either. But if you'll take me through boarding one step at a time, I'll do the same for you at the wall. I've done it with other people — helped them climb a little higher each day until they can do it all by themselves."

"Does that really work?"

"Give me two weeks and we'll find out."

X thought for a moment. "All right, but on one condition. Tell Alison the truth first."

Ben groaned. "Okay," he said. He glanced at something over X's shoulder, then back to X. "But I've got a condition, too. Stop letting everything Frank says gnaw at your brain."

"Deal."

"Starting now," Ben said.

"Well, well, well, if it isn't Chicken Boy," Frank drawled from behind X.

X shot Ben an I'll-get-you-for-this look.

"Know what I heard?" Frank said. "I heard that chickens don't fly because they're afraid of heights." His friends snickered. Frank smiled like he'd just said the funniest thing in the world.

X narrowed his eyes. "You talk awful big for a guy who was standing *outside* the rope circle at the wall. How's about we meet *inside* the ring in, say, two weeks" — he winked at Ben — "and see who makes it to the top of the wall." He grinned. "I dare you."

Frank turned red. Then he shoved past X and disappeared down the hill. His friends looked at one another.

"Come to think of it," the girl said to the boy, "I've never seen Frank climb up anything higher than this hill. You?" The boy shook his head. "Huh. Oh, well. C'mon, let's shred." They *swished* down the slope after Frank.

"Nicely done," Ben said as he watched them go.

X knocked fists with him, Jonas, and the rest of his friends. "Rock on," he replied.

How to Start "Rockin' On"!

Rock climbing is a challenging sport that requires balance, concentration, and courage. Climbers study the rock face closely before beginning a climb. During the climb, they focus on each movement, taking great care to be sure each foothold and handhold is secure before moving on. For most climbers, the goal is to reach the top of the cliff — but how they get there is just as important.

People new to rock climbing should try bouldering first. Bouldering is fairly simple and doesn't require any special equipment beyond sneakers or hiking boots, comfortable clothes, and a big boulder. To boulder, climb up a few feet, then cross the rock face from one side to the other and back again. For safety's sake, never go bouldering alone — and choose a boulder that has little or no debris around its base. Loose rocks, sticks, and underbrush can be hazardous in the event of a fall.

While bouldering may seem tame, it allows beginners to practice looking for and using handholds and footholds. Without these skills, a climber won't be prepared to tackle bigger challenges. Those who feel ready to move on – and up! – should join a rock-climbing club or take lessons through a local outdoor sporting-goods store. With the right equipment and help from experienced people, beginners will move safely upward to exhilarating new heights!

THE TALE OF
TOM KITTEN